JN077370

おばさんから子どもたちへ
贈る言<ruby>の葉<rt>こと　　は</rt></ruby>

Collected Coupling Poems of Japanese Two Women Poets
In English & Japanese (Vol.2)

From Aunties to Children
A Gift Of Singing Poems

白石かずこ ・ 水崎野里子
Kazuko Shiraishi & Noriko Mizusaki

ブックウェイ

白石かずこ詩集：目次
Collected Poems of Kazuko Shiraishi Contents

水崎野里子詩集：目次
Collected Poems of Noriko Mizusaki Contents

白石かずこ

Kazuko Shiraishi

卵のふる街

青いレタスの淵で休んでいると
卵がふってくる
安いの　高いの　固い卵から　ゆで卵まで
赤ん坊もふってくる
少年もふってくる
鼠も英雄も　キリギリスまで
街の教会の上や遊園地にふってきた
わたしは両手で受けていたのに
悲しみみたいにさらさらと抜けてゆき
こっけいなシルクハットが
高層建築の頭を劇的にした
植物の冷い血管に卵はふってくる
何のために？
＜わたしは知らない　知らない　知らない＞
これはこの街の新聞の社説です

EGGS FALLING DOWN ON THE TOWN

When I have a rest on the edge of a green lettuce leaf,
Eggs come falling down.
Cheap and expensive ones, from hard ones to boiled eggs.
Babies come falling down,
Boys come falling down,
So are rats, heroes, and even grasshoppers,
They came down on churches and playing parks.
Though I was receiving them on my open palms,
They sliding through them down, like sadness did.
A funny silk hat falling down,
It turned the top of a skyscraper, so dramatic.
They came falling down on cold blood vessels of the plants.
For what purpose?
< I do not know. I do not know. I do not know.>
This goes a leading article of the newspaper in this town.

(Translator: *Noriko Mizusaki*)

終日　虎が

終日
虎が出入りしていたので
この部屋は
荒れつづけ
こわれた手足　や椅子が
空にむかって
泣いていた
終日
虎　が出入りしなくなっても
こわれた手足　や椅子は
もとの位置を失って
ミルクや風のように
吠える
空をきしませて　吠えつづける

ALL DAY LONG: A TIGER…

All day long
A tiger was coming in and out,
This room
Gotta messy.
Broken limbs, an' destroyed chairs
Cry loud
Up into the sky.

All day long
Now even though he is gone away,
The broken limbs, the destroyed chairs
Deprived of their original spots,
Together with milk and winds,
Keep howling on.
They still howl, screeching the sky.

(Translator: *Noriko Mizusaki*)

9

10月のセンチメンタル・ジャーニー

あなたは　10月の月だ
あの顔のない満月
らいらくな笑いが　たそがれの方から
やってくると
あなたの　若さは　急速に　年老いる
センチメンタル・ジャーニー
あなたの恋は　鰐のように口をあいて
今、歯を磨いている
その白い歯に
あなたの日々が　ちいさなウソ
ちいさな真実となり
どちらも栄養よく
ツヤのある　幸な光となって　とまる

あなたの大きい目をもってしても
この10月の　ボーバクから吹いてくる唄
（センチメンタル・ジャーニー）のメロディは　みえないのだ

しかし　あなたは　きくだろう
メリーゴーラウンドのように　まわる　まわる
あの　快楽の木馬のシッポが　あなたの
シッポの雄々しさに　よく似ることを
メリーゴーラウンドも
すべても
まわる　幻影だ

だが

IN OCTOBER: MY SENTIMENTAL JOURNEY

You are a moon in October,
The full moon with no face.
Your laughter nonchalant comes heard,
Around from the dusky evening,
When, your fresh age goes rapidly aged.
Oh! My sentimental journey!
Your love opens a mouth like a crocodile does,
Brushing the teeth.
Your days perch on the white teeth,
In the shape of tiny lies,
Or tiny truths,
Either of them looks well-nourished,
Shiny, happy light.

Even with your big eyes
You cannot see the melody of the (Sentimental Journey),
The song comes blow from the wild vastness of this October.

But you will hear
A tail of a rocking horse for pleasure,
That circulates on and on like a merry-go-round,
Just looks like the manly bravery of your tail.
The merry-go-round and
Everything else: all are
Rotating fantasies.

But

あなたも　わたしも
まわらない
ただ　すぎていくのだ
満月をよぎる雲の
粋な　そぶりとなり
あ、10月の月
顔のない満月がある
名前のない存在
あなた　が　ある

You and me
Do not go round,
Only go passing by.
Like the clouds that go passing,
Over the full moon: How nice!
Look! The moon in October!
A faceless the full moon, there!
The nameless presence,
There you are!

(Translator: *Noriko Mizusaki*)

星

「はずかしいの」ときいた
ことことと箱の中で音がした
いきいきといきがかよって
春のおぼろ月夜のような冬の月
氷がべったりとあたしを抱きしめてくれる
霧が酔っぱらってくちづけしにきた
じっとしていると
またききにきた
「はずかしいの」
あたしの目はおもたく
星の方へひらいていった

A Star

"Are you shy?" asked a star to me.
The hitting sounds in a box, I heard.
Taking lively breathes, I regained,
The winter moon up like a hazy moon in the spring.
The ice gave me a hug, tight and sticky.
The mist, tipsy, came to kiss me.
I stayed still,
Then the star came again to ask me.
"Are you shy?"

Heavy eyes I had,
Started opening to the star.

(Translator: *Noriko Mizusaki*)

ハドソン川のそば

誰から生まれたって？
ベッドからさ　固い木のベッドから

犬の口から骨つき肉が落ちたように
落ちたようにね

わたしの親は　まあるいのさ
月のようにのっぺり
やはり人間の顔してたのさ
人間の匂いがしてたのさ

くらやみの匂いがね
だまってる森の匂いがね

それっきりよ　ニューヨーク
ハドソン川のそば

わたしは立っている

この川と　わたしは同じ
流れてる

この川と　わたしは同じ
たっている

広すぎてはかれないよね　おまえの胸幅
遠すぎてはかれない　おまえの記憶

BESIDE THE HUDSON RIVER

You asked me, who I was born from?
From a bed, from a wooden bed so hard.

Just like a bone-in meat dropped from a dog's mouth,
Just like it dropped down.

My parent is just round,
Just like the moon with no features.
But still, she had a human face.
She had a human scent.

You know, it is a scent of darkness,
A scent of silent woods.

Only for that, in New York,
Beside the Hudson River.

I am standing.

This river is the same with me:
Flowing.

This river is the same with me:
Standing.

You are too large to measure your chest,
You are too far to measure out your memory.

生まれた頃まで　さかのぼることないよ
わたしの想い出
行先も今も　ただよう胸の中
自分でも　はかれないのさ

ハドソン川のそば
ちぢれっ毛の
黒い男の子　やせて大きな目だよ　わたしは

笑うと　泣いてるように
顔がこわれて　ゆれだすよ

唄うと　腰をくねらせ
世界中が　腰にあるように　踊るんだよ

名前はビリー
すぎた日の名は知らない

わたしの生まれた　空を知らない
なんていう木か　死者のハッパが　あったか　なかったか

わたしの生まれた　うまごやを知らない
ワラのベッドか　木のどこか

それでも　わたしはそだった
果実の頬のように
果物屋の　店先で
買えない果物みてるうち

ハドソン川のそば

You do not have to trail back to my birth.
My memory,
The future as well as the present, drifting in my bosom,
Even I cannot measure.

Beside the Hudson River,
Having curly hair,
A black boy I am; skinny, with big eyes.

When I laugh, as if I weep,
My expression broken and starts trembling.

When I sing a song, I will start dancing,
Twisting my hips, as if I have a whole world, there.

My name is Billy,
I do not know my name in my days passed.

I do not know the sky, when I was born. Not knowing,
What the tree is called. Whether it had leaves for the dead or not.

I do not know my stable where I was born.
I was born on the straw bed? Or somewhere in the tree?

Though,
I have grown up,
Just like cheeks of fruit,
Which I watched at the grocery,
Penniless.

ひとりで　いまはたつ

すこしおとなになったわたしかかえ
わたしのグランマー　グランパー

いとしい恋人　ハドソン川
わたし　流れていくだろうよ　川と一しょに
わたしの胸の中　太く流れるハドソン川と
わたしの胸の中　わたしと流れるハドソン川と

Beside the Hudson River,
Alone, I stand now.

You are holding me, a bit grown up.
My Granma! Granpa!

My dear love, the Hudson River!
I shall go flowing together with you.
In my mind, you always a big river.
I have been living with you, so shall I do.

(Translator: *Noriko Mizusaki*)

サックスに入って出てこないアル

アル　は
サックスの中に入って
でてこない

夜が来て　男たちは
ステージに立ったが
アルだけは
荒らい音をかかえたまま

少女のように　そのくらがりに
ひそんでいる

女は　客席をこわし
ビールを割る
サックス　を空にぶつける

と
星たちに　かかえられて
サックスは　アルの手足をふきはじめる

AL LURKED IN THE SAX AND NEVER COMES OUT

AL
Crawled into a sax,
Never comes out.

In the night,
Men stood on the stage but
Only AL was
Holding rough sounds in his arms.

Staying still in the darkness,
Like a girl.

A woman destroyes her seat,
Breaks a bottle of beer, and,
Flings the sax against the sky.

Then
Rocked by stars
The sax started to blow AL's limbs

(Translator: *Noriko Mizusaki*)

23

ライオンの鼻歌

わたしは昨日ライオンだったので　密林で
鼻唄をうたっていました　夜には
星が一せいにふりだしたので
月の光をふみつけては
いたるところやけどをしました
鼻の頭をすりむいたり
恋で生命をあぶなくこがしたり
また　たてがみは風に吹かれて
過古　未來　死　何処へともなく
永遠にとび去ったのです
わたしの尾も耳も
もはや二度とわたしの所へは帰って来ますまい

今日　学校の帰り
わたしは鏡屋の前を通りました
それでこれだけは憶いだしたのですが
ピンセットを密林に忘れたので
二度と鼻唄の文句だけは
つまみだすことができません

HUM OF A LION

I was a lion yesterday, so in a jungle,
I was humming a song. In the night,
Stars started falling down, all together,
Stepping on their light,
I got burned every part of me.
I got scraped on a top of my nose,
Or for my love, I would have scorched out all my life.
Besides, my mane was blown away in the wind,
All flew away: to the past, to the future,
To death, or to somewhere else, forever.
My tail and ears shall never come back
Again to me, I am sure.

Today, on my way back from school,
I passed a mirror shop.
Then I remembered only that,
Because I left a pair of tweezers in the jungle,
I could not ever pick up
My hum's words.

(Translator: *Noriko Mizusaki*)

25

アル　と　ホルン

黒人の大男のアルは
ホルンの中で眠っていた

風は森にいない
この部屋に　花がない
女に　唇がいない
黒人の大男のアルは
ホルンの中で　もう
めざめることはできない

アルの腕はホルンのかたちに
伸びていった
アルの足　はホルンの外に見えない音のリボンになって流れていった
そして　ほんとに黒人の大男アルの胸は
ホルンの外の真空の壁になってしまった

AL AND HORN

AL was sleeping in a horn.
He was a black man, so big and tall.

No winds in the woods.
No flowers in this room.
No lips women have.
Never can he wake up, in the horn.

In a horn's shape,
His arms grew stretching,
Like ribbons of invisible sounds,
His legs were flown away out of the horn, into the air.
His black and really large chest, driven away from the horn, too,
Transformed into a vacuum wall, skipped out of the horn.

(Translator: *Noriko Mizusaki*)

犬と男

犬は裏庭で
男は玄関で　よぶ
＜おなかがすいたのです＞
＜とても逢いたいのです＞

男は玄関で
犬は裏庭でなく
＜愛がほしいのです＞
＜とても哀しいのです＞

男と犬が
どちらが哀しいか
おなかがすいたことと
愛のないことと
どちらが　つらいのか

神様
あなたの答は　何ですか

A DOG AND A MAN

A dog at a backyard,
A man at an entrance hall, calls loud.
" I am hungry!"
" I want to see you!"

The man at the entrance hall,
The dog at the backyard, cries,
" I need love!"
" I am terribly sad!"

Who is sad,
The man or the dog?
Which is painful,
You are hungry, or
You want love?

My dear god,
What is your answer?

(Translator: *Noriko Mizusaki*)

白石かずこ（しらいし　かずこ）

1931年カナダのバンクーバー生まれ。早稲田大学第一文学部演劇科卒業。詩人、翻訳家、エッセイスト。ロッテルダム国際詩祭など海外文化交流・海外詩祭に参加多数。H氏賞、イスラエルやセルビアの詩祭など、国内外の詩祭・団体にて受賞多数。詩集・著作多数。

十代から詩を書き始め、北園克衛の「VOU」に所属。北園に師事した。早稲田大学文学部大学院在学中、二十歳の時に詩集『卵のふる街』を上梓。現在、東京杉並区西荻に居住。

1960年代から70年代にかけて、日本の詩人たちの間で、詩の音声朗読とジャズの統合イベントの試みと開催があった。72年春の渋谷のデパートの駐車場で開催されたイベントが聴衆800名を集めた大イベントであった。参加詩人は吉増剛造、諏訪優、佐藤文夫、八木忠栄、村田正夫など今でも有名な詩人の中に、白石かずこの名も見える。ジャズ側は沖至四重奏団、今田勝など。サンフランシスコの画廊で詩の音声朗読を始めたアメリカのケネス・レクスロスやジャック・ケラワックなどアメリカのビート派詩人の影響と受容に、日本のジャズ音楽家の活動を合体させた活動であったが、この活動の中で、白石かずこの独自の朗読スタイル、あるいはパーフォーマンスは独特であり、個性が光っていた。女史は、奉書に毛筆で書かれた詩を読みながら音声朗読していった。「勧進帳」の一名場面を思い出させる。女史の独創性と国際性を示す。

Kazuko Shiraishi

Born 1931, in Vancouver, Canada, she graduated from Waseda University, in Tokyo, majoring Drama, in the Drama Department of the First Literature Faculty, and studied in the Graduate Course. A poet, essayist, and translator. She was invited or participated in the famous poetry festivals; as Rotterdam Poetry Festival and others, abroad as well as in Japan, which are counted so many. She was awarded with so many prizes, in Japan, Israel, Serbia, and others, including Mr. H. Poetry Prize, in Japan. She published so many books, of poems, essays, and translation works.

She started writing poems, in her teens. She published her poems, in "VOU." It was edited and led by Katsue Kitasono, who is still the one of famous Japanese poets, as international.

At the age of twenty, when she was a university student, she published her first poetry book, *A Town Eggs Falling On*. Now, in the present, she is living in Nishiogikubo, Suginami-ku, Tokyo.

From the nineteen sixties to the seventies, in Japan, not a few Japanese poets had the joint events of poetry with jazz music. One of them, outstanding, to be remembered, was held at the parking lot of a department store in Shibuya, Tokyo, which had eight hundred audiences. The poets who participated in it, were Gozo Yoshimatsu, Yu Suwa, Fumio Sato, Chuei Yagi, Masao Murata, who were all outstanding poets, then, with leading roles, and, Kazuko Shiraishi.

Those Japanese jazz musicians, were the Oki Itaru New Jazz Quartet, Masaru Imada, and so on. It was a cultural activity, influenced by the poetry activities, which were started by the poets, so-called the beat generation, in USA, like Kenneth Rexroth, or Jack Kerouac, who started oral readings in such a place, as the gallery in San Francisco. And at the same time, it was joined by the Japanese jazz musicians, at the time. Kazuko Shiraishi was outstanding in this kind of activities, in another words, in the kind of performances, which led her to the creative and unique stages abroad and domestic. She devised the kind of the oral recitations, reading poems, choreographed or written, on the rolling paper, in the ink brush: now called a reading style of the hosho paper, the thick and soft traditional Japanese paper of high quality, rolled. Her way of the recitation reminds us of the one dramatic scene of Kanjincho, one of the most popular and traditional Japanese kabuki play, .It shows originality as well as internationality, of the poet, which should be noted down.

(Translator: *Noriko Mizusaki*)

水崎野里子

Noriko Mizusaki

ファンタジア

私は小さな女の子
あなたは小さな男の子
二人でお手々繋いで
蓮華の花咲く野原を
駆けて行きましょう

石ころはパンに変貌する
泥水はきれいな飲み水に
枯れたキャベツは　割れて二人のお布団に
金色キャベツの　金色クッション
雲さん下りて二人を包む

イモムシさんは銀の鍵
秘密の花園　入り口開ける
二人は入る
秘密の花園
世界の変貌

あたしたち
小さな女の子と男の子
ふたりのために　世界はあるの
お花の咲いたきれいなお庭を
お手々繋いで　一緒に走る
大人になってもまだ走る

Fantasia

I am a tiny girl,
You are a tiny boy.
Let's hold hands together,
And go galloping,
In the field, full of spring flowers.

Stones will transform into bread,
Muddy water, into clear drinking water.
A withered cabbage will divide into halves for our beds,
They will have turned golden: golden cushions.
Clouds will have come down to mantle the couple.

A worm turns into a silver key,
It unlocks the secret garden.
They enter it,
The garden of mystery.
There, the world should have been transformed.

We are a couple of
A tiny girl and a tiny boy.
For us the world exists.
Holding hands together, we go galloping,
In the garden, full of flowers in a full bloom.
When we become grown-ups,
Still we shall go running together,
There, holding our hands.

(Translator: *Noriko Mizusaki*)

カルメンの歌

なんでまた
あたしの前に
薔薇の花
髪に挿したら
あたしカルメン

ほら　あんた
あたしと一緒に
歌って踊ろう
愛も　明日も
どうでもいいわ

あたしの人生
宙に跳ぶ
チンタオの
ビールほろ酔い
ギターは撥ねる

あたしの上に
ネズミが走り
あたしの上に
空がおっこちる
あたしの人生

めちゃくちゃ人生
薔薇の花　髪に
真っ赤な　踊り

A Song of Carmen

Why is it then?
Before me
A rose flower
Putting it into my hair
I am a Carmen

Hey you!
Together with me
Sing to dance!
Love or tomorrow
I do not care

My life does
Jump up into the air
Beer of Jindao
Made me tipsy
The guitar sounds give me leaps

Over me
Rats race
Upon my head
A sky tumbles down
My life is

A messy life
A rose flower for my hairpin
I dance a scarlet dance

あたし　爆弾
真っ赤な　爆弾

歌と踊りで
あんたを爆破
あたし　カルメン

赤い薔薇

I am a bomb
A scarlet bomb

Singing and dancing
I'll explode you!
I am Carmen

A red rose

(Translator: *Noriko Mizusaki*)

九月

深い深い　ところから
ぼうばくの風が吹いて来る
九月
ぼうばくの　Septemberの中に
ひとのからだの存在感を　思ったが
私は既に他のことを考えている

破けた黒コウモリを開くと
ぼうばくの九月の色が見えるだろう
九月の色は
Bo Boと流れて行くだろう

Bo Boと歌うと
私もぼうばくになるのだ

Bo Bo Bo Bo
ぼうばくと一緒に吹きながら
ぽけっとに手を入れたり出したりするうちに
九月は一緒に出たり入ったりするかもしれない

Bo Bo Bo Bo

A September Song

From someplace in the depths,
An autumn wind comes blowing: elusive like a vast wilderness.
Now I am in September,
In the vast and elusive month.
I thought of the sense of existence
Of our human bodies,
But now I am thinking of something else.

When I open my broken umbrella,
I see the color of September.
It will
Go flowing: blowin' and blowin'

When I sing the blowin' song,
I become vast and solitary.

Together with the blowin' September,
I am blowing, too,
Putting my hands in and out of my pockets.
So September may do,
Together with me.

Blowin' and blowin'

(Translator: *Noriko Mizusaki*)

41

星々の間を

星々の間を歩く
あたりは透明な水色
両足を動かさなくても
すいすいと前へ進む

小さな孤独を抱きしめて
ここを歩くのは楽しいわ
軽やかな足取り
軽やかなこころ
もう　知らない
地面に釘付けされたあなたのことなんて
私は　今　軽やかな　ひとりぼっち
地上では　あなたと私は　目隠しの鬼ごっこ

突然　星たちが輝き出し
私は　星たちの胸に抱かれる
どしゃぶりの雨の中
星たちと踊る
激しいリズムの　ロックダンス

でもここは束の間の休息
星たちはいるけど　冷たい輝きばかり
もうすぐ　私は地上に帰る
そして私は口紅を塗りたくって
繰り返すつもり
とめどもない　たましいの鬼ごっこ

WALKING IN THE STARS

Now I am walking in the stars.
Here, in the transparent air, all over,
Blue, mantles me.
Without moving my legs,
I can walk forward on and on.

Cherishing a tiny loneliness,
Walking up in the air I enjoy.
My steps light,
My heart no heavy.
I am away from you,
With no cares for you,
Who has got nailed down onto the ground.
Now I am alone, high up the ground,
Where you and me were playing a tag game,
Blindfolded.

Suddenly,
The stars started twinkling bright.
They hug me in their bosoms.
In the pouring rain,
I start dancing with them,
Rock dances in the passionate beats.

Though,
For me, this is my short rest.
Staying with stars,

But all they have are icy twinkles,

In the morning,

I am getting down to the earth,

Then,

Putting on a rouge on my lips,

I shall repeat, endless,

The tag game together with you,

Seeking for the soul, each other.

(Translator: *Noriko Mizusaki*)

たましいを探して

河を上って
わたしの
たましいを
探しに行く

波は
きらきら光る
たくさんのうろこ
風に
ゆらゆら
そよいでいた
その間を
わたしのたましいが
ピョンピョンと
生きのいい
おサカナみたいに
たくさん
泳いでいた

わたしは
虹色した
網を
投げ
たましいを
いっぱい
捕まえた

SEARCHING FOR SOULS

I rowed
Up a river
Searching for
My souls

Waves were
Like so many scales
Of fish
Glittering
In the breeze
They swayed
To and fro

Among them
My souls were
Swimming
So many
Like fishes
Jumping
Up and down
Fresh and
Lively

I did
Throw away
The fishing net
And caught

逃げないように
きらきらの
水滴で
光る
網で
がんじがらめにした

たましいたちは
うろこだらけの
金色の
川面で
お魚みたいに
虹色に
きらきら
光った

So many of
My souls

Not for them
To escape
I did
String tight
All of them
With the net
When
The water drops
Twinkling down

My souls
Shined bright
In the color of
A rainbow
Just like fishes
On the water
Golden and
Full of scales

(Translator: *Noriko Mizusaki*)

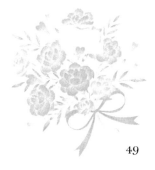

怒涛の河

怒涛の河があった
私たちは下った
三人で　一艘の筏で
命を賭けた　全力で
越えた　ずぶぬれになった
着いた　下流の　乾いた岸へ

人生は　怒涛の河
男は救った私を　怒涛の河から
私は救った男を　男の子供を
怒涛の河から　無法者から
三人で下った　荒れ狂う河

新しい生活　愛
もう私は　戻らない^{ノーリターン}

＊本詩の原案は1954年にリリースされた米国の映画、「帰らざる　河^{リバー・オブ・ノーリターン}」(邦名)
である。オットー・プレミンジャー監督、フランク・フェントン脚本、スタン
リー・ルービン制作。ロバート・ミチャム、マリリン・モンロー主演。
私は若いころ、この映画を見たて感動した。粗野な男たちが金鉱を求めてやっ
て来る。喧嘩、争い、決闘、発砲、騙し合いと賭博。アメリカ原住民の攻撃。金
鉱、イカサマ、無法者、原住民の襲撃、下積みの女。映画は開拓時代のアメリカ
をよく表現していた。マリリン・モンローが主役の女ケイであり、しがない酒
場の歌手をよく演じた。彼女は、だが、優しいこころを持ち、ひとりの少年の面
倒を見ている。彼の父親はいなくなった。(殺人で刑務所にいた)。ある日、彼は
戻って来る。ケイの元恋人も帰って来る。筋は巧みである。賭博で金鉱を手に
入れたというケイの元恋人。イカサマか？　彼を追う無頼の男たち。原住民の
襲撃を避けやがてケイ、少年、彼の帰って来た父親との三人、筏で下流の街へ、
怒涛の河を下る。街ではケイの元恋人と少年の父親は決闘となる。危機一髪、
少年は背後から敵を撃ち、父親を助ける。父親の不在は実は、かつて決闘で友
達を救うため、背後から敵を撃って殺した。そのため刑務所で服役していたと
彼は息子に告げる。三人は元の農場に戻り、新しい生活を始める。

THE RIVER OF TORENTS

There was a river of torrents.
We flowed down the river,
By three people, on a raft.
Dangers we passed through.
All drenched, then, arrived
At the city, down the river.

Life is a river of torrents,
A man saved me from the river,
I saved him and his boy, too,
From the river of anger,
From outlaws, lawless men.

For a new life, and new love.
I will return, no more.

* This poem was some hinted by the U.S. movie, "The River of No Return." released in 1954.

When I saw it in my young days, I was deeply impressed with the movie production. Rough men, seeking for the gold mines, with fights, duels, shootings, deceiving and gambles. Native Americans often attacked them: In the movie, Marilyn Monroe had a leading role, who acted well a singer of rough bars, though, tender-hearted. She loved a boy and took his cares, while his father was away. One day, he came back. One day, her former lover came back, too. The story was brilliant and made up so dramatic. The boy shot a man from behind, to save his father, who, once shot his enemy from behind, too, to save his friend, he said. Probably he stayed in a jail, for the punishment, which he confessed to his son. At the end, the three people came back to their farm in the mountains, to start a new life together.

(Translator: *Noriko Mizusaki*)

アフリカ

ふらふらと
いつものなじみの街角を曲がると
アフリカだった

アフリカ！
たくましく白い乾いた平原
燃える灼熱と原始の力を
押し倒し叫ぶ濁流

呻く太陽を
吸い込み消化する
砂漠の熱さ

視線は遠く吸い込まれ
駆け回り　繰り広げる
血みどろの生の闘い
血は走り　血は叫び
灼熱の太陽

夕陽が沈む
彼女はあかがね色に染まり
走り行く　あかがね色の砂漠の中を
聞こえる　どこからか
雄々しく　静かな　砂漠の合唱

彼女は走る
髪に汗と太陽が染み込み

AFRICA

Casually, when I happened to
Turn at the familiar street corner,
I was in Africa.

Africa!
The Savanna plain is stout, white and dry,
Dashing torrents are roaring loud,
Hush down the heat : the primitive energy.

The desert is heated,
Inhaling to digest
The hot groaning sun.

Sights are absorbed into the far horizon,
Animals galloping around the plain,
The bleeding fights for survival.
Blood runs. Blood screams.
The hot and scorching sun.

The sun sets.
She is dyed in orange color,
She runs on and on, with no ends.
Then she hears, from somewhere,
The chorus of the desert, majestic,
Yet so quietly sung.

She runs on and on,

アフリカの落日が彼女の着物だ

ふらふらと
いつもの街角を曲がると
アフリカだった
私は歩いているのだった
もうすぐそこに家がある
信号は　赤

Her hair is soaked with sweats and
The setting sun is her gown.

Casually, when I happened to turn
At the familiar corner of streets,
I was in Africa.

I was walking on a roadside,
On my way back home.
My house is just there.
The signal is red.

(Translator: *Noriko Mizusaki*)

私が少女だったとき

１．吉祥寺のジャズカフェ

吉祥寺の駅前にあった
南口　それだけ
もうどこか忘れた
狭い階段を上った
まだ慣れなかった　珈琲の　味
流れていた　サキソフォン

今は失われた　カフェ
背伸びした少女の
大人のなり始め
曲の名は知らない　演奏者の名前も
知らない　でも知らずに
少女は　ジャズを纏って
大人になった

無名のサックスの音
叫んでいた　吠えていた

２．ピット・インにて

これもだいぶ前の経験だ
ジャズ喫茶　ピット・イン
新宿　でも　新宿のどこにあったのか
もう　記憶にない

When I was a Teenager

1. A Jazz Café in Kichijoji

All I remember now is that:
It was situated somewhere just near to
Kichijoji Station, a short way from the south exit.
A narrow stair I climbed up,
The taste of coffee bitter, for me,
Sounds of the saxophone and other instruments
Filled full in the small space.

Now it is lost: the café
There staying was on the first stage
For me, in the course of growing-up.
I did not remember who played,
Nor who sang the songs.
Though, wearing jazz
I became a grown-up.

The sounds of saxophones:
They were shouting, screaming loud.

2. PIT-IN

This memory was on another jazz café.
I visited not a few times, in my young days,
It was called, PIT-IN,
Situated in Shinjuku, Tokyo. But,

気取った素振りの　東京の街
懸命に気取ったつもりの　少女
サックス　苦い珈琲　煙草の煙

次々と聞こえてくる　ジャズ
少女は首を伸ばす　未知の世界
わからなかったくせに！
と　大人になった私が言う

わかったふりをしていただけよ！
と少女の私が言い返す
でも　そこにいるだけでよかったのだ
夜の東京　疾走する豹　大きな象さん
サックス
喧噪の音楽　芸術とは喚くことだ

Exactly where it was mapped in Shinju,
I have no memory at all, now.

Tokyo looked pretending to be smart.
Following it, I, a girl, was trying hard,
Having the pose, pretending the smartness;
The saxes' music sounds, cups of coffee,
Smokes of cigarettes;
Jaz music came played one after another.
I stretched myself up, as hard as I could,
Towards the unknown music.
"You did not understand them, did you?"
Said I, who had grown up into an adult.

"I just pretended I could have appreciated!"
Answered I back, as a girl. Though,
Only sitting in the café was good enough for me.
Tokyo in the evening, a puma dashes: so big an elephant nose,
The sax was.
The sounds played loud, so high toned, to be called as clamors.

Art is to shout. Shout in anger.

(Translator: *Noriko Mizusaki*)

言葉

ああ　神！
言葉を与えたまえ
水のように
雨のように

大地をしめやかに濡らし
あなたの心を共に濡らす
言葉を
大地の幻影を

誰も見えない時
私が私に語りかける　その時
私のどこかで紅いバラがぽっと開く
そんな
たった一言の言葉を

WORDS

Oh, my dear god!
Give me words,
As, just like water,
Or rain,

Would wet the earth quietly,
As well as your heart.
Give me such words,
Reflections of the earth.

When I am alone and lonesome,
When I have to mutter to myself,
Give me your words,
As if a red rose suddenly would pop out.
Such words,
Even in a short phrase.

(Translator: *Noriko Mizusaki*)

水崎野里子（みずさき　のりこ）

1949年東京生まれ。早稲田大学第一文学部英米文学科大学院修了。演劇科でも学んだ。詩人、翻訳家、エッセイスト。マケドニア・ストルーガ詩祭、世界詩人会議など海外詩祭に参加多数。イスラエル、インド、モンゴル、カリフォルニア世界詩人会議優秀詩人賞、日中韓平和功労賞など海外詩祭・国内団体で受賞多数。詩集『二十歳の詩集』他、著作刊行多数。幼年時は武蔵野市吉祥寺に住んだ。杉並区にある都立西高校卒業。現在は千葉県に居住。

水崎の場合にも、海外詩会を含めれば、パーフォーマンスを含む詩の音声朗読（英語と日本語で）の経験はかなりある。奉書に代わる日本性は、和服、浴衣着用、時には扇子を持った。千葉県詩人クラブと現代詩人会共催の詩人会では、和服姿で舞台上に座り、自由詩「坂」を暗唱音読した。新型落語のつもり。ストルーガ詩祭での開会式では、舞台上に浴衣姿で座り、ライトの中で短歌をバイリンガルで朗唱（歌唱）した。現代詩人会の韓国・ソウル大会では、韓国楽器演奏をバックに日本語で詩を音声朗読した。アメリカ翻訳者会議では夜のデクラマシオンという会で、だいぶ（十年間くらい。2020年はコロナで延期）、短歌を日英両語で朗唱（歌唱）させていただいた。同じく和服姿と扇子。専門テーマは世界のマイノリティの文化と詩。翻訳に『現代アメリカ黒人女性詩集』、『現代アジア系アメリカ詩集』他。
参加者の国籍を問わない多言語誌「パンドラ」主催。米国カリフォルニア本拠ズーム詩人会POV会員。

Noriko Mizusaki

Born in 1949 in Tokyo, a poet, essayist, and translator. She graduated from Waseda university, in the First Department of Literary Faculty, in the Department of English and American Literature Studies, then she finished the Graduate Course. She also attended the seminars on the drama. During the doctoral course, she lived in Boston, Massachusetts, USA, attending the classes and seminars in MIT and Harvard. She published not a few essays and poetry books, like *Poems at the Age of Twenty*.
She also participated in,such international poetry festivals so many, as Struga Poetry Evenings in Macedonia, and local congresses of the World Congress of Poets. She was awarded with prizes international, in Israel, India, Mongol, California, Korea, and China, as The BESETO: The Best Poet Prize for Peace and Arts.
In her young days, she lived in Kichijoji. She graduated from the Metropolitan Nishi High School, which is situated in Suginami-ku. Now she is living in Chiba.

In her case, too, she attended so many poetry festivals or congresses abroad, outside Japan, as well as inside Japan, for the oral recitations of poems, in English and Japanese, which sometimes can be called as performances, including bilingual singing with some kind of gestures, though in her cases, she used to wearing kimono, or yukata (kimono for the summer), sometimes with a fan: in the joint congress of the Chiba Poets Club and the Japan Poets Association, at the time when Makoto Ooka was the president, following a new style of a rakugo, a comic talk of monologue. And in the opening ceremony of the Struga Poetry Evenings, in Macedonia, where she sat just on the stage, in a Japanese way: legs folded, and recited a tanka poem first in English, then sang it, in Japanese, spot-lighted so bright. In the Japan Poets Association International Exchange with Korea, which was held years ago in Seoul, Korea, she recited a poem in Japanese, accompanied with Korean musicians at the back, who played Korean traditional instruments, during her readings, so well.

In the same Kimono style, in US, in the annual conferences of the american literary translators association, in the declamacion, a poetry recital at night, they gave me the waka recital occasions, in bilingual, with singing in the waka way in Japanese, for about these ten years.
Her main theme is on the minority people's culture and poetry, in the world.
Her translation works: *The Contemporary American Black Women's Poetry, The Contemporary Asian American Poetry. etc.*
She is editing PANDORA: a bilingual book for poets: annual publication. A Member of POV ZOOM Poetry Meeting: the host home in California.

(Translator: *Noriko Mizusaki*).

終わりに

白石かずこ・水崎野里子

みなさん！　おばちゃんの詩を読んでくれてありがとう！
世界にはいろいろな子供たちと大人たちがいます。
すべてのひとびとがしあわせで楽しい毎日を過ごしているとは限りません。
病気や戦争に苦しんでいる人もいます。貧困や嵐や地震に苦しんでいるひともいます。
人生には苦しいことも楽しいこともあります。でも負けないでまっすぐしあわせに生きてください。希望をいつも持ってください。
このご本は日本のおばちゃん二人のあなた方世界の子供たちに贈る花束です。
世界にはたくさんの人々がいます。皮膚の色は白、黒、黄色、褐色とさまざまです。
みんなきれいな色です。みんな平等です。いじわるな人がいても負けないで下さい。

2021年春

After Words

Kazuko Shiraishi & Noriko Mizusaki

Hi! All of you! Thanks for your reading our poems to the last one!

In the world various children and adults are living along.

But it is not that all of us are always living happy and merry days.

Some of us suffer from sickness or wars. Some people live in hardships from poverty and the natural disasters like storms and quakes.

You have to live through difficulties and hardships, while you can have a right to live in happiness.

Do not get defeated by them and live straight and in happiness. Always you do not forget hope.

We are two aunties living in Japan. This book is our present to you, all the children in the world, for peace and hope.

In the world, so many people are living, with a variety of skin colors: white, black, yellow, and brown.

All of them are beautiful. All people have equal human rights. If someone should bully you, not be defeated to live.

Spring, 2021

日本女性2人詩集（2） おばさんから子どもたちへ　贈る言の葉
2021年7月15日　初版発行

著　者　白石かずこ、水崎野里子
発行所　学術研究出版
〒670-0933　兵庫県姫路市平野町62
[販売] Tel.079(280)2727　Fax.079(244)1482
[制作] Tel.079(222)5372
https://arpub.jp
印刷所　小野高速印刷株式会社
©Kazuko Shiraishi, Noriko Mizusaki 2021,
Printed in Japan
ISBN978-4-910415-20-8